HENDRIX THE ROCKING HORSE

For Debbie

First published in 2016
by Faber and Faber Limited
Bloomsbury House
74–77 Great Russell Street
London WC1B 3DA

Designed by Faber and Faber
Printed in China

A CIP record for this book is available from the British Library

978–0571–31540–6

2 4 6 8 10 9 7 5 3 1

Gavin Puckett

Illustrated by Tor Freeman

ff

FABER & FABER

Hello young reader . . . !

Thanks for taking the time,
in selecting my book of ridiculous rhyme.
I'm Gavin, (you'll find my full name on the cover)
the teller of tales, which you're soon to discover.
It's taken me years to unearth these strange fables,
by visiting farmyards and hanging round stables
– and this is a series with just a selection, of some of the weirdest in my collection.

They're all about horses – each one of them true,

and it's such a nice privilege to share them with you!

Well, when I say *"True,"* I mean . . . that's what I've heard.

(It's hard to believe, since they're all so **absurd!**)

So, instead of returning this book to the shelf,

why not read on and decide for yourself?

Hendrix was raised on a West Country farm,

in a spot quite well known for its *elegant charm.*

The town was called Higgleston; a picturesque place,

full of mythical tales and historical grace.

It had quaint, RUSTIC COTTAGES
painted in white
with neat, little flowerbeds, pretty and bright.
But Hendrix found Higgleston
frightfully dreary –
the silence around him just made him feel weary!
He'd wake up each morning and stare from his hill,
at the quiet, old town standing peaceful and still.

There was NOTHING TO DO except

stare at the sky –

or occasionally gaze at a car passing by!

"I wish *something* would happen."

he'd say, feeling blue.

Then one summer's morning . . .

HIS WISHES CAME TRUE!

As he rose from his bed, Hendrix

rubbed his tired eyes,

then gazed down the hillside and

gasped with surprise.

The meadow beneath him had

changed overnight . . .

to a **BUSTLING FAIRGROUND** and festival site!

HIGGLESTON MUSIC FESTIVAL

There were marquees, a **Ferris wheel**, fair rides and stalls.

There were people on stilts that were juggling balls.

There were stages – all sizes – for different events

and the green fields around him were covered with tents.

Hendrix felt giddy, his heart was a flutter.

"WOW!" was just about all he could utter.

He had never seen anything like it before,

he clapped his small hooves and was keen to know more!

His hillside provided an excellent view,

so he sat on the grass in the mid-morning dew.

Hendrix stayed there all day

(without any persuasion)

nibbling grass on this special

occasion.

Higgleston was truly a *sight to*

behold

and Hendrix grew eager to watch

things unfold.

That evening the Mayoress appeared on the stage,

she was **eighty years old** (but looked good for her age!)

The sweet lady waved with her frail, little hand,

before *tottering* up to a microphone stand.

"Welcome!" she said in her calm,

gentle voice,

"To our first music festival – let us rejoice!"

Then she put down

her handbag, hitched up

her frock,

and screamed to

the crowd . . .

"ARE YOU READY TO ROCK?"

The whole place erupted and then came a sound,

so loud and **ferocious**, it shuddered the ground.

The stage became foggy and lights started flashing –

followed by drumbeats and loud cymbals crashing.

The audience cheered, their arms began swaying

and suddenly, onstage . . .

A band started playing!

"We're the **TUMBLING PEBBLES!**" yelled the singer aloud,

over the roar of the clamouring crowd.

Their first song **EXPLODED** – distinctive and raw,

with guitar riffs that left the fans yearning for more.

These musicians

oozed talent – they

breathed rock and roll

and each song was

bursting with rhythm

and soul.

"FANTASTIC!"

squealed Hendrix with

joy and elation,

and looked on,

hooves tapping in
sheer admiration.

He boogied and
whistled and sang
without care,

to the
music that
pounded the
summertime air.

Next morning, as Hendrix peered down from his hill,

he was met with a vision that made him quite ill.

The party was over, he felt heavy-hearted,

as slowly but surely the people departed.

Hendrix mooched through the meadow and cantered on down,

to one of the fields on the outskirts of town.

Then he stopped at a fence by a telephone mast

and gloomily watched all the people drive past.

But just as the horse was about to turn round,

his ears became drawn to a *rumbling* sound.

The strange sound grew louder,
and louder – until,

he spotted a bus on the brow of the hill.

It was totally black and impeccably clean;

with a paint job that sparkled a glossy, bright sheen.

Each of its windows was stylishly tinted and the wheels were so polished, they glimmered and glinted.

Just then (as it eased into cruise-control mode),

from nowhere, a cat darted into the road.

The poor driver *shrieked* feeling rather unnerved –

he *slammed* on the brakes and he frantically swerved.

The cat scurried off to a field where it hid,

but the bus juddered sharply and *started to skid!*

The wheels clipped the curb, the vehicle jolted –

and the rear door sprung open, as the door-lock unbolted.

Then, in all of the panic, the fuss and commotion . . .

Something fell out while the coach was in motion!

But the bus didn't stop, it still thundered along,

with the driver oblivious to what had gone wrong.

Hendrix HOLLERED again, but despite his persistence,

he watched as it powered off into the distance.

The curious horse had a quick look around

then he sniffed at the object that lay on the ground.

It was luggage – all black, with a hard plastic shell

which was fitted with clasps and a

handle as well.

He carefully picked up the case by his

teeth

and he noticed a label was stuck

underneath.

The paper was tatty and looked rather

old,

but a name and address stood out,

clear and bold.

It said . . .

PROPERTY OF: THE TUMBLING PEBBLES.

with a scrawl that read . . .

No 1 Musical Rebels!

Underneath that, it said . . .

Hendrix leapt up and cried out in delight . . .

"It's the **Tumbling Pebbles** . . .
The band from last night!"

But what was inside . . .?
He hadn't a clue!

Now, there was only
one thing left to do.

After studying both of the latches

intently –

he fumbled a little, and opened them

gently.

When he lifted the lid up the horse

nearly died,

in TOTAL EXCITEMENT

at what was inside.

Its body was **'V'** shaped and painted

bright red,

with a long rosewood neck and a small wooden head.

It had six metal strings that were evenly spaced,

and a strap that was crafted from leather and lace.

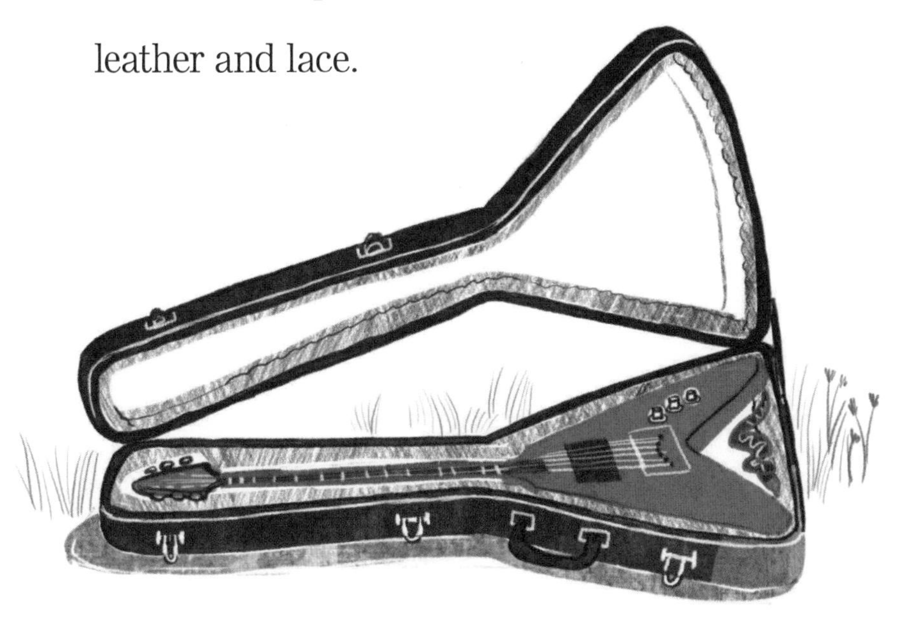

"WOWZERS!" said Hendrix,

"An electric guitar . . .

and one that belongs to *a real rock star*!"

There were other bits too – musical things;

like song sheets and plectrums and packets of strings –

plus a crinkled,
old folded up
magazine page,
with a shot of the
Tumbling Pebbles
onstage.

The singer was photographed clenching
his fist,

wearing colourful scarves round his
head and his wrists.

The other three members looked cool as can be.

"AMAZING!" said Hendrix, exploding with glee.

Then the horse saw – (by a small tambourine) – **a recording device** with a digital screen.

Hendrix picked up the item, all compact and neat.

It had three small, round buttons:

RECORD - PLAY - DELETE.

He checked out

the object, but wasn't

impressed –

it looked rather **boring**

compared to the rest.

So he tossed it back in, without

hesitation

and focused once more on his 'six-

stringed fixation.'

Hendrix was nervous, but
nevertheless,
he plucked at a string with a gentle
caress.

His heart skipped a
beat – his adrenaline
surged
when a gentle
melodious echo
emerged.

That's when it happened – the horse lost control,

as the sound reached inside him and tickled his soul.

He sensed an emotion he'd not had before;

a reaction that bubbled and fizzed from his core.

I'd call it an urge; (it was all quite bizarre)

and his very bones whispered . . .

PLAY THAT GUITAR!

So, that's just what he did! With a grunt and a neigh,

Hendrix picked the thing up and he started to play.

At first he was cautious and found it quite strange; but it didn't take long for that feeling to change!

He strutted and bounded and stylishly twirled,

feeling totally lost in his own little world.

He strummed and he twanged with a steady, rock beat –

and at that very moment . . .

The horse felt complete!

(Now as you read this, it's quite clear to me that you're obviously wondering . . .

How can this be? I know there's a question that niggles and lingers . . .

How can he play if he hasn't got fingers?

It really does seem an impossible task;

it's a question indeed that I too

had to ask.

So rather than keep you in further

suspense;

I'll tell you – then hopefully all will

make sense!)

Guitar players pick with a plectrum

or thumb,

or a *sliding technique* is a preference

for some.

Well . . . horses have hooves,

(It's just one of those things)

and their hooves sound **INCREDIBLE**

sliding down strings.

When Hendrix stopped rocking, *(five hours later)*

his passion for music had grown

EVEN GREATER!

He thought of the festival, closed

both his eyes

and imagined spectators with whistles and cries.

He pictured them punching their fists in the air,

as they sang to his music and danced without care.

"THANK YOU HIGGLESTON!" he yelled, with his happy face beaming,

"I'M HENDRIX!" he roared, as he stood there daydreaming.

Then amid his mad musings and imaginary cheer,

Hendrix the horse had a brilliant idea!

The horse went to work leaving *no time to waste*

and he drew up some posters and banners with haste.

He galloped to town and put some on the wall,

of the churchyard, the school and the local town hall.

They read . . .

HIGGLESTON TOWN
HAS A NEW RISING
STAR!
COME WATCH HIM
PLAY ON HIS DAZZLING
GUITAR!

Below that it said . . .

DO YOU WANT TO ROCK?
THE FARMYARD,
THIS SATURDAY –
SEVEN O'CLOCK!

Hendrix couldn't wait to take
stage and perform
and knew in his heart, he would go
down a storm.
He had FIVE DAYS to practise
until the big night
and would not let his instrument
out of his sight!

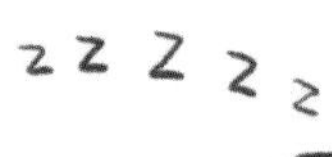

Hendrix slept
with it, ate with it,
washed with it too –
even carried it

with him
to go to the loo!

By Wednesday, the
usual stillness and calm,
was replaced by an
energised buzz round the
farm.

The streets were alive – and

wherever you went,

you could hear people talk of this

mystery event.

On Thursday, when Hendrix got

out of his bed,

he went for a walk (to clear his

head).

When all of a sudden, there whistled a breeze

that blustered around him and rustled the trees.

Then up blew a newspaper page from the ground;

it fluttered and floated and danced all around.

The horse felt the blood drain away from his head

when he saw what the newspaper

article said . . .

The Tumbling Pebbles have quit read the caption . . .

After precious guitar goes missing in action!

It told of a band member – Ron was

his name,

who had guided the **Tumbling Pebbles**

to fame.

But now, with his wonderful instrument gone,

there was no way that Ron and the band could go on!

With his head in his hooves and his thoughts in a mess,

Hendrix fell to the ground in a state of distress.

He now found himself in a terrible tiz – having suddenly realised . . .

THE GUITAR WASN'T HIS!

He stayed there for *hours*, just thinking things through.

"Oh my!" sobbed the horse, "What on earth should I do?"

He faced a dilemma – all centred upon . . .

Should he keep the guitar . . . or return it to Ron?

After hours of painstaking thought and confusion,

Hendrix had finally reached a conclusion.

He remembered the feeling of joy and delight,

when he first heard **'The Pebbles'** that festival night.

To let them split up would be simply unfair;

it was clearly something he just couldn't bear . . .

and so, with a sorrowful look on his face . . .

Hendrix put EVERYTHING back in the case.

Early next morning, the horse left his shed,

knowing the rest of the farm were in bed.

Then . . . when the Higgleston postman took mail to the house –

Hendrix crept to the post van,

as quiet as a mouse.

With the case in his teeth, Hendrix opened the door

and he placed it inside on the carpeted floor.

He stood there and watched with a sad, heavy neigh

as the postman came back and the van drove away.

But soon . . . Hendrix froze with a horrified fright – and yelled . . .

When Saturday evening
eventually came,
Hendrix the Rocker just wasn't
the same.
His confidence and feelings of
utter elation
had changed overnight to a sense
of deflation –

and to make matters worse – the
WHOLE COUNTY had flocked,

to come see this mystery figure that
rocked.

The Mayoress stood proud in the
very front row –

she was keen to establish the star of
this show.

There were kind volunteers who'd
formed a small crew

and constructed a stage with a lighting-rig too!

So – even if Hendrix was riddled with doubt,

it would be too late now for this horse to pull out!

But his dreams had since faded; his future seemed bleak,

for without that guitar he felt hopeless and weak!

“What am I to do?” he cried in frustration

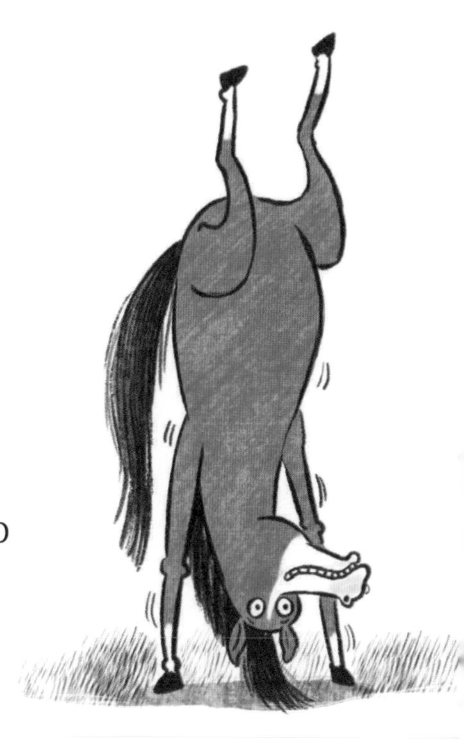

and searched in his mind for a *spark of creation.*

"Perhaps I could tap dance . . . or stand on my head . . .

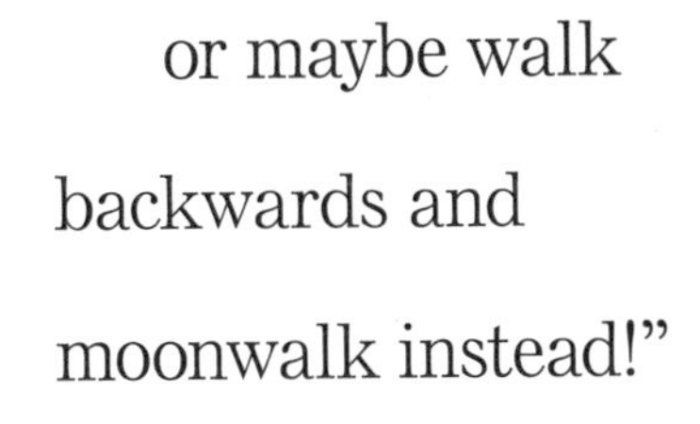

or maybe walk backwards and moonwalk instead!"

(He had once seen a racehorse do this on the news –

with significant help from his back-to-front shoes!)

But . . .

There was no time for Hendrix to learn any moves,

or fuss about fiddling with shoes on his

hooves.

So he thought of the **Tumbling Pebbles**

once more

and pictured the cool, stylish clothing

they wore.

He dashed to the farmhouse as quick

as can be,

being careful that none of the others

would see.

The weather was fine, (not a cloud in the sky)

and the farmer's wife's washing was pegged out to dry.

"Fantastic!" said Hendrix, "Those will do fine!"

As he studied the clothing that hung on the line.

The farmer's wife, Audrey, was in her house cooking

and Hendrix could see there was nobody looking.

Then, at the same super-speed that a lightning bolt flickers,

he snatched *two long socks* and a *pair of red knickers.*

With one or two knots and a few
clever twists,

he tied both the socks on to each of
his wrists.

He held up the knickers,

"PERFECT!" he said –

and he pulled Audrey's underwear on
to his head.

Without

his guitar, then

the second best

thing

would be

dressing up

stylishly . . .

READY

TO SING!

Hendrix felt butterflies deep in his belly,

his head was a mess and his legs were like jelly.

He ambled on stage to the cheer of the crowd,

who were very excited and keen to be wowed.

Now when the crowd saw him the cheering all stopped;

some of the spectators' mouths even dropped.

They had hoped for a rock star – yet somehow instead,

they now had a farm horse with pants on his head!

But before his first song even took off the ground,

from nowhere, there came a strange **rumbling** sound.

"What is that noise?" said the crowd, all a fuss.

Then suddenly . . .

Up pulled a very large bus!

The windows were tinted, it was shiny and black

and it stopped by the stage on a small, windy track.

"It can't be!" said Hendrix – his
mind full of doubt,

as the tour-bus door opened – and
four men walked out!

They wore colourful headscarves
and rock-star-like suits,

each with tight leather trousers
and big cowboy boots.

Hey dudes!

"It's the **Tumbling Pebbles**!" someone yelled with a cheer,

"But what are they doing and why are they here?"

The Pebbles approached as Hendrix gazed on.

Then one of the band said, "Hi, Hendrix, I'm Ron!"

The horse appeared shocked . . . How on earth did he know?

Had they come all this way to watch Hendrix's show?

Then Ron gave a smile and he cleared his throat,

before pulling a camcorder out of his coat!

"Uh?" grunted Hendrix, rather

confused,

"That's the one from the case!" he

said, feeling bemused.

(It was the same device Hendrix had

previously seen –

the one with the **buttons** and

digital screen!)

Hendrix simply didn't know what

to say

as he stared at the screen after Ron

had pressed play.

He saw himself playing that

wondrous guitar –

with the swagger and flair of a

rock 'n' roll

star.

“But how?” asked the horse, as the Pebbles applauded,

(he was desperate to know how they had this recorded!)

Then everything suddenly fell into place . . .

It switched on . . . when he’d tossed it back in to the case!

“You’re a talent!” said Ron, “And you have quite the knack!

But I'm ever so grateful you gave my stuff back."

Hendrix now nodded and let out a neigh,

he was glad that the instrument found Ron OK!

"We've got something for you," said Ron with a grin,

"It's just to say thank you for doing the right thing."

Hendrix's mind was entirely blown, when Ron gave the horse . . .

A GUITAR OF HIS OWN!

It was stylish and curvy and painted bright blue

and as soon as he held it . . .

He knew what to do!

Hendrix swaggered and strummed, he bounded and twirled

and was once again lost in his musical world.

In *seconds*, the whole place was

rocking and jiving –

the Mayoress got up and she started

stage diving!

The crowd, (who went crazy) all
started to yell,
so the **Tumbling Pebbles** joined
Hendrix as well!
The concert continued for most of
the night
and the horse who told me found it
a remarkable sight.

As for Hendrix the horse, (well,
I'm sure you know)
he went down in history – as the
star of the show!

I suppose in the end, what they
say must be true . . .

When you choose to do good . . .
Something good will find you!

MUSICAL PASSION!

COMING SOON . . .
COLIN
the Cart Horse